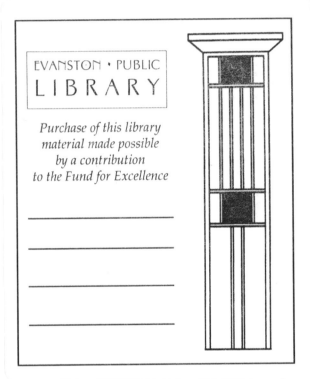

I'm Still Standing

Angela D. Evans

authorHOUSE®

AuthorHouse™
1663 Liberty Drive
Bloomington, IN 47403
www.authorhouse.com
Phone: 1-800-839-8640

First published by AuthorHouse 6/28/2010

ISBN: 978-1-4520-1912-3 (e)
ISBN: 978-1-4520-1911-6 (sc)
ISBN: 978-1-4520-1910-9 (hc)

Library of Congress Control Number: 2010906184

Printed in the United States of America
Bloomington, Indiana

This book is printed on acid-free paper.

"Hi, Margaret."

"Hi, Ann. How are things going?"

"Well I won't complain. I'm blessed, and I let God do the rest."

"That's a good model. You know, it's amazing how much you've gone through and still you stay in good spirits."

"That's the only way I can be. You see, what you know is only 1 percent of what I've come through. You see me lying here, but that only means that God is still in charge."

"If it was me, I would be crying nonstop and asking the Lord to end all of this."

"I've done that in the past, and God decided that I should stay here a little longer. You see, a lifetime for us is less than a millisecond to him."

"Okay, tell me how you came to be in the mindset that you're in now."

"To do that, I have to take you to my beginning. Yes, my birth. You see, I was born in a small room. We lived in the Prince Street Projects. My mother always reminded me throughout my youth that I was born the night of the riots in Newark. She said that I must have come from hell because it was as if Newark went to hell that week. The ambulance came after I was born. They checked my mother and then me. It took over an hour for us to get to the hospital because we had to dodge fires and rioting. But we made it there.

"As I grew older, my mother got hooked on heroin. I started daycare at two years old because my mother knew the owner and I was toilet trained. I remember. I know it sounds unlikely, but I can remember staying after all the other kids left. I would play by myself."

"Your mother picked you up late?"

"No, she came on time, but she would always go in the back and stay until it was dark. Once we left, she would take me to get ice cream. I came to like staying late because I would get that ice cream afterwards.

When I turned five, I no longer went to the daycare because I was in school. One day, my mother and I went back and visited the daycare. She said if I was quiet we would get ice cream. We hadn't done that in a long time, so I was excited. There was another boy there. He was probably twice my age. He had candy and offered to share it with me. I thought, *Wow this is great; I get candy and ice cream.* After my mother had been gone for some time, I got tired. I lay down. I fell asleep. I don't know how long I slept. I woke up to something hurting me between my legs. That boy was on top of me, and I noticed he had taken off my underwear. I was wearing a dress. I tried to push him off, but he said this is what grownups do. I told him to stop, that I didn't like it. He said if I relaxed I would like it. I tried to do what he asked and then cried out, 'Stop! It hurts!' Just then my mother came out. She looked at us and said, 'I knew you were too grown. I'm going to beat you when we get home." When we got home, she spanked me. I didn't even get my ice cream."

"I can't believe she did that."

"That was my mother. After that, she started leaving me at home alone. When I was ten, she started getting sick. She said it was my fault."

"Why?"

"Because if she didn't have me, she could have a husband and wouldn't have to work. She said that she went with a lot of men in order to take care of me."

"I can't believe you went through that."

"That wasn't anything. When I was twelve, she looked so worn from the drug use and being sick all the time. At that time, we didn't know about HIV. She looked really bad; men didn't even want her to perform oral on them. So to keep our apartment, she asked me to take care of her 'John.' I couldn't believe that she was serious, until one night I heard her on the phone telling someone to come over. It was Mr. Roberts. He used to come over a lot until my mother started getting sores all over her body. Before he got there, she made my face up and put some of her sexy clothes on me. She told me to be good and to listen to what I was told to do. She also demonstrated on a banana what I should do if asked to perform oral sex. I didn't cry because I was so shocked. I was actually numb. When Mr. Roberts came over, she brought him in my bedroom. I can still remember. I was sitting on my bed, still in a daze and trying to think of how to get out of doing it. Mr. Roberts came in and looked at me. He saw how young I was and refused to have any part of tarnishing my youth. He gently smiled at me, reassuring me that he wouldn't hurt me. I guess he knew that my mother would blame me, so he gave her the money he usually gave her when she had sex with him. For a while, I guess he did it to protect me; he would come by and leave us enough money to pay rent and buy groceries. Many times, I still went hungry because my mother would use the food money to buy drugs. I guess I should be happy that she paid the rent."

"That was nice of him."

"Yes it was. This went on for two years. When I was fourteen, Mr. Roberts was robbed and killed after leaving our apartment. As weak and as sick as my mother was, she insisted on going to the wake and funeral. We went, and even though he wasn't related to us, I felt such a loss, as if he was my father. I know that sounds strange, but I knew if it wasn't for him, my mother would have had men in and out of our apartment and I would have had to service them. That night I cried all night.

"The next morning, I got ready for school. My mother wasn't up. I was surprised because she was always up when I had school. She always checked to see if I was up. I called out her name, but she didn't answer. I found her and shook her, but she didn't move. I ran down the hall to this old lady's apartment—she used to come by to check on us. Her name was Miss Rosie. She came down the hall as fast as her eighty-year-old body could bring her. She checked my mother and then told me that my mother was just sleeping hard. I was relieved. She told me to go to school. I lightly kissed my mother, thanked Miss Rosie, and left for school.

"When I returned home, Miss Rosie was in our apartment, sitting on our worn-out couch. I asked her where my mother was. She told me that she had to call the ambulance, and I began to cry. She told me which hospital my mother was taken to and said that I had to be strong. I ran out of the house and kept running until I reached the hospital. I went to the receptionist's desk and gave them my mother's name. I found the room they directed me to, and when I walked in, my mother looked so small lying in her bed. When the doctor came in, I lied about my age. So he gave me her prognosis. She was in a coma and wasn't expected to come out. She was a charity case, which I didn't know at the time meant she was getting the minimum treatment. She died three months later.

"Miss Rosie did what she could to help me, but I was fourteen and on my own. I got Miss Rosie to front for me to stay in the apartment. I tried to get a job, but no one would hire me. When I got the notice of eviction, I went out on the street begging. I would go to places where I didn't think anyone knew me. I would say that I was lost and trying to get home. I dressed in a Catholic school uniform so people were more inclined to give me more money than they'd give a beggar. After a while, the people started remembering me, so the money decreased. I did that for a year."

"Miss Ann, you look tired. Rest. I'll come back to check on you tomorrow."

"Okay."

Ann tossed and turned before getting comfortable and drifting off to sleep. She liked sleeping because of her vivid imagination; she had wonderful dreams. She used to try to make herself sleep so she could escape.

* * *

The next morning, Margaret came in to check Ann's vitals. Then the doctor came in. After doing his routine check, he talked to Ann for a few minutes and then left.

After the doctor left, Margaret said, "So continue your story."

"Are you sure you want to hear about my life?"

"Yes."

"Where did I leave off? Oh yeah, well after a year of begging in nice areas, I decided to go over to New York. I dressed up the same but didn't do as well over there, so I changed my look and tried to look homeless. This got me more sympathy, which increased my collection. One day, a young girl—maybe a couple of years older than me, a very pretty, young, light-skin black girl with beautiful hair—came up to me. She asked, 'Why do you beg? You can make a lot more money.' I thought she knew about a job. Well I guess she did, just not what I had in mind. Her name was Candice. I'm sure that wasn't her real name, but I didn't know it at the time. She knew a lot of people. She took me to an abandoned building where I couldn't believe young women were going in and out with men.

"The outside of the building was brick, sturdy, and marked up by graffiti, but inside it was fixed up. If I hadn't known better, I would have thought people lived there. There were beds, not messy, actually kept neat. Candice told me that a pretty girl like me, if I dressed the part, would be able to make a lot of money and wouldn't have to beg. I was sixteen then. I was tired of begging and didn't want to be hungry anymore, so I asked her how I could do it. She said that she would bring me in. The head of this prostitution ring—what they called an organization—was twenty-three. She had been out on the street since she was twelve. She was pretty, didn't do drugs, and on one occasion showed us a picture of her house. It was beautiful. I thought, *Wow, I would like to have a place like that.*

"So I decided to do it. I was still a virgin. The only encounter was with that boy when I was five. I would go over to New York every day after school. The girl, or I guess you can call her madam, set up our Johns. My first time, I went dressed as a schoolgirl. The man was probably in his early twenties. I couldn't believe he would need to pay for sex because he was a good-looking man. I pretended that he was my boyfriend and that we were in love. We didn't kiss. He said, 'Hi.' I said, 'Hi.' He asked my name. I hesitated, and then thought I'd make up a name. I said, 'Melondy.' He said, 'That's a pretty name.' I guess he was trying to make me feel more comfortable; I suppose I was showing that I was nervous. He began to take off his clothes, and I could see that he was already aroused because his penis was erect. I couldn't stop staring at it because I had never seen one before. I think he saw the fear in my face. I thought he was pretty big even though I had never seen one; I was sure that his was exceptional.

"He was gentle though. He told me to come over, and he patted the bed. I slowly walked over and sat beside him. He told me to touch it. I shakily placed my hand on it. He put his hand over mine and started moving my hand back and forth to show me how it should be done. I could tell he was getting excited because he laid back and moaned a few times. He then told me to put my mouth on it. I just put my lips on it. He said, 'Not like that.' He didn't yell. He was very patient. He told me how I should do it, and that excited him even more. I guess I was doing it right because he kept saying yes. Soon it was over. At that time, I didn't know what this stuff was, but in time I learned. Afterwards, I thought, *Okay, that wasn't too bad, I can do this.* For a while, he was the only John that I had. Eventually he progressed to wanting vaginal sex. He was my first. It was painful but not that unpleasant. You see, I had formed this relationship in my mind about this guy.

"After a couple of months, he stopped coming and others replaced him. They were nice, but it felt a lot different. I felt dirty. I actually longed for the first John. I found out a year later that he was really my pimp and was the main reason most of the girls came into the

9

business. This was his routine. In my distorted mind, I still thought that he had feelings for me, and I lounged for his touch.

"I finished school and thought of going to college, but making the money that I began to make made me go deeper into the system. I wanted to retire early and live nice and have all the things that I had dreamed about while growing up. I opened a bank account the day I graduated high school and started prostituting myself full time. After two years, it began to get to me. I had quite a bit of money in the bank, but I hated the way I felt after every job. I brainwashed myself to think it was just a job. I was good looking; I exercised and had a great body. I was good at what I did, but when regular guys approached me, I couldn't bring myself to talk to any of them. I know it sounds crazy, but I thought that I was cheating on Charles. Yes, that was his name. I fell in love with him. I guess because he was my first. I thought he would come back, but he never did. I made money for him and myself and Candice who was his bookkeeper. I have to admit, it was a great set up. I stayed in the business for five years. I purchased a home in the suburbs. After five years, I started getting tired and depressed. I wanted someone to love me. I was twenty-one.

"I signed up for college. This took me to part-time status. I was able to get full tuition, but I had to keep up my expenses, so I still needed the business. I made enough to keep up on my bills and still had a sizable bank account. I met this guy in college; he was in one of my classes. He was drop-dead gorgeous— 5'11", light skinned, beautiful hair that he wore back in a ponytail. He was Native American, Black, and Asian. He was so nice. He started out by opening the door for me. He sat next to me. We would speak.

"One day after working all night, I went home, showered, and only had a few hours of sleep before having to go to class. When I arrived at school, there was a note saying that the class was canceled. My next class wasn't for two hours. I didn't want to go and come back. He asked me if I wanted to get something to eat. So I went. His name was Mark. I can still remember him as if it was yesterday. After that, we began to talk when I wasn't working. This occurred mostly in between classes. We officially had our first date two months from the class closure. We went out a few times and then ended up dating. I decided that I would give up the business."

"He must have been a great guy."

"He was. I was falling in love and didn't realize it. Let me see, it was a month after I had given up the business when Mark and I went to a movie and then out to dinner. He gave me a look—a look I was familiar with. But it was a more sensual look, not just wanting to do me. I was turned on. I didn't know that was possible. After leaving the restaurant, we walked a few blocks to a nearby park. We walked hand-in-hand and sat on a bench and talked. He told me about his past, and I changed the subject when we got to mine. He told me his dreams, and I told him about mine. As it got late, he dropped me off at home. Although I wasn't a virgin, in a very strange way, I didn't want him to get the wrong idea of me." Ann chuckled. "Can you believe that? Me not wanting a man to get the wrong impression."

"I can understand. You were changing your way of life."

"Subconsciously. We would go out, talk on the phone, and kiss. But I would always pull away. I really didn't know how to act. Before, with the Johns, they told me what to do, and I wasn't trying to be anything but what I had become. With Mark, I had decided I wanted respect. This was my first boyfriend, and I wanted to be courted. We went on like this

for six months. Then one night I invited him to come over. I decided to make him dinner. He came over and was impressed with my house. I let him believe that it had been left to me. After dinner, we relaxed on my couch. We talked. We kissed. I could tell he was nervous. I let him lead being the man and all.

"I couldn't believe how he made me feel whenever we were together. When he touched me, I got so turned on. After a while of kissing and touching, I led him up to my bedroom. He made me feel so good that I called out his name." Ann laughed and shook her head.

"I had called men's names out in the past, but it was always a performance. I held onto him. He must have felt my excitement because he tensed up and whispered my name. He kissed me on my lips, and we held each other all night. We drifted off to sleep, not waking until morning. The next day was Saturday, and we spent the entire weekend together—eating, talking, cuddling, talking about our future, and making love.

"Six months later, he moved in. We graduated college, me with a bachelor of arts degree and Mark with a criminal justice degree. Can you believe it—I became a teacher. Mark became a sheriff's officer. We had a good life together. There was only one thing that was missing."

"What was that?"

"A baby. We were so in love, but I couldn't carry a baby full-term. I got pregnant a few times, but I miscarried. You see, back when I was prostituting, the first time that Charles and I had sex I became pregnant. I hid it for a while before I started to show. By that time, I was too far along to have an abortion. I still worked up until my ninth month. After I had the baby, I thought of giving up the business. But then my mother's words rang in my ear blaming me for our struggles and for her not finding a husband. I had nothing, and I didn't want to torture my own child with the same sentiments. Baby, I'm tired now."

"I'm sorry. Get some rest. I'll come back." Margaret fixed the pillows behind Ann's head and then turned out the light as she left the room. Margaret finished her shift and went home.

***

When Margaret entered her home, she heard the pitter-patter of footsteps running from the second floor.

Her three-year-old daughter Ana came running down the stairs and said, "Hi, Mommy!"

Margaret bent down and picked up her baby girl saying, "Hi, baby."

The housekeeper followed behind Ana. "Hi, Margaret."

"Hi, Doris. How was Ana?"

"Perfect. She's a good girl. Well I'll see you in two days."

"Okay."

Doris left, and Margaret fixed dinner. After she and Ana ate, Margaret put Ana to bed. The next morning, they went to the hospital.

Ana asked, "Where we going?"

"To see a nice lady who's very sick in the hospital," Margaret said.

When they entered the room, Ann was sleeping.

Ana said, "Is this the nice lady?"

"Yes. But you have to be quiet."

"Okay, Mommy."

Ann soon opened her eyes. She looked over and saw Ana first. She looked disoriented as she said, "Baby girl."

Ana said, "Look, Mommy, she woke up."

"I see, baby."

Ann looked at Margaret, smiled, and said hello.

"Hi, Ann. I thought we'd come by to see how you were doing."

"You're so nice, coming to see me on your day off. You know, for a minute I thought I was looking at my baby girl. You see, after I had my baby girl, I tried to take care of her, but I was young. I gave her to be adopted when she was one year old. It broke my heart. But I knew she was going to a good person. She was good people—a beautiful little girl. She looks like that little girl. If I didn't know any better, I would swear she was her."

"This is my little girl Ana."

"What a nice name."

"I thought you would like it."

"After the couple adopted her, I went back to work. I worked when I wasn't in school. People talked about me, but I ignored them, and if someone asked me where the baby was, I told them that I sent her upstate to relatives. I cried every night for a year after the adoption. After that, I got on the pill. In the beginning, I used to forget to take them sometimes. I had to get a few abortions because I didn't want to have children all over the place, and I couldn't bear giving another baby up. After my third abortion, I began taking my pills like I was supposed to. After me and Mark got married, I stopped taking the pill. I was in good shape, so I couldn't understand why I couldn't carry a baby to full term. I rested and prayed. But for some reason, I couldn't hold on to my babies. For a while, I thought that maybe it was a punishment for giving up my baby girl or for not having the other three. But I've accepted my fate and pray for forgiveness every day and night. I just hope that my baby girl knows why I gave her up—if she knows she's adopted."

Ana became fidgety.

"Well, Ann," Margaret said, "I think I better get Ana home. She's getting restless."

"Okay, baby. You get that baby home. Be safe, and thank you for bringing your daughter to see me. I don't have any family. It's nice to have someone visit."

"I like talking to you and listening to you talk. I'll see you tomorrow. I have a double shift."

"That's nice. See you tomorrow."

When Margaret and Ana left, Ann closed her eyes and quickly fell asleep. She began to dream. *She was out at a party, dancing with Mark. He held her close, and they danced all night. After the party was over, she looked around and realized they were at home. She told him that she was pregnant. He was so happy. He picked her up and swung her around. That night, while making love, he kept asking if she was okay and wanted to make sure he wasn't hurting her.* Ann woke up smiling, still amused at his behavior. She could still feel the warmth of his touch, and she held herself, basking in the memory.

That night, when Ann went to sleep, she dreamt about her mother. *Her mother was taking her to school. She was about ten years old. She looked up at her mother, thinking how pretty she was and how she wanted to be just like her. All the men liked her mother. As they got closer to the school, her mother began to be further away from her. She tried to walk slower, but it didn't help. When she made it to the school building, her mother was so far away she could barely see her. She turned to walk back to her mother, but her mother moved backwards until she disappeared. She ran inside of the school and tried to tell her teacher, but no one would help her. She was then in her apartment, getting ready for her mother's funeral. When they got to the church, she walked up to the casket and looked in. She smoothed her hand over her mother's face. As Ann went to kiss her mother, she closed her eyes. When she opened her eyes, she saw herself in the casket. She moved back and closed her eyes. When Ann opened them again, she looked up; she was lying in the casket. She struggled to wake up.*

Ann woke to Margaret lightly shaking her. She opened her eyes.

Margaret said, "Are you all right?"

"Yes. I'm fine. I was just having a bad dream."

"Would you like a drink of water?"

"Please."

Margaret poured the water and helped Ann hold the cup. Ann was still shaking.

"That must have been a really bad dream," Margaret said.

"It was kind of scary."

"So other than your dream, how are you today?"

"I'm doing okay."

"How's the pain?"

"It's not too bad. Before I had the scary dream, I was dreaming about Mark. It was the night I told him I was pregnant for the first time. He was so happy. I can still remember it as if it was yesterday. I so wanted to give him a baby. But I never did."

"Where is Mark?"

"He died a few years ago."

"Were you still together?"

"Till death do us part. We took our vows seriously. I guess you're wondering if I ever told him about my past. The answer is yes. You see, Mark was a wonderful man. When he asked me to marry him, I couldn't believe someone actually loved me enough to want to spend the rest of their life with me. So before I answered him, I told him my life's story from my birth up until the time I had met him. I never thought that my past would prevent him from having a lineage. After I told him, he sat for a few minutes and then said, 'So will you marry me?' I sat there. I couldn't believe that he still wanted me. I said yes. We were inseparable until the day he died." Ann's eyes clouded with sadness.

"Are you tired?" Margaret said. "Do you want me to let you get some rest?"

"Rest. That's all I do. No, I was just thinking that once more my past caught up with me. He died from complications due to AIDS. You see, during my time on the street, I didn't practice safe sex. How ironic. I took birth control but didn't make my Johns strap on a condom. Its' amazing how you try not to be like your parents, but in some ways, no matter how hard you try, you repeat their habits. But you know, he never seemed angry or bitter. Whenever I would beat myself up about it, he would comfort me and tell me he didn't regret being with me. On his deathbed, he told me that he loved me more than life itself and that he'll be waiting for me on the other side. He gently smoothed his hand over my face. He urged me to bend down, and he gave me the most loving kiss that you can imagine. Then he died. Because he gave me so much love and he was in so much pain, I had the strength to go on. I miss him every day and long to be with him again one day."

"Were you sick then?"

"You know, I wasn't diagnosed until maybe two years after Mark got sick and was diagnosed. At first I was afraid that he was going to die; it would be my fault, and I didn't get sick. I know it might sound crazy, but I was almost relieved when I was diagnosed as having AIDS. I wanted to go with him. I know God has a purpose for all of us, and I know that God wanted to bless me—and he did the day he brought Mark and me together."

"That's so nice to hear."

"Well, miss lady, you've picked my brain about my life. Are you married? Do you have a man?"

"There's not much going on in my social life," Margaret said. "I've never been married, never been asked. I was dating Ana's father for three years and thought maybe we would someday get married, but he never asked. We had been dating for a year when I got pregnant. Two years went by and no word of marriage. I asked him about it one day, and he said that it was my fault that I got pregnant and that he knew I was trying to trap him. We broke up that night. I was so hurt and decided I was wasting my time with him. He's an attorney, does well for a living, but I don't think he'll ever get married. Some people aren't the marrying type. He visits the baby and helps take care of her."

Margaret notices Ann dozing off. She said, "Ann, I'm going to make my rounds and then come back to see you later."

"Okay, baby."

When Ann fell asleep, she dreamt about her husband. *They were sitting on a porch, looking out at a lake. Ann was sitting in front of her husband, and he had his arms around her waist. She felt so secure. They watched the boats come and go. As the boats came in, people got on them. They seemed so happy.*

Mark said, "Well I need to find out first."

She felt his hands leave her waist. Mark gently kissed her.

Ann said, "Where are you going?"

"You'll see me soon," she said.

In an instant, she saw him go onto the boat, and the boat disappeared. Ann got up and yelled, "Wait for me!" But the boat had left.

She began to cry in her sleep. She woke up and saw Margaret standing over her saying, "Ann, are you all right?"

When Ann regained her composure, she said, "I'm fine. I was dreaming about Mark. It was beautiful—then he left me. I yelled for him to wait, but I guess he couldn't. You know, no matter how hard this life is, we still don't want to leave."

Margaret said, "I know what you mean."

"Enough of that talk. It was nice seeing Mark again. He looked like he did when we were just married. He was a wonderful man. I had some struggles, but God blessed me the day I met Mark. You know, sometimes God lets you go through certain things so you know how to appreciate when things are good in your life."

"Well I guess God has a lot of good things stored up for me," Margaret said.

"I don't know what you've been through, but look at that beautiful little girl you have. That's one of those good things I'm talking about. Maybe that baby's father didn't turn out the way that you wanted, but God's got the man for you. Just wait and see."

"I hope so."

"Ain't no hope. You just wait."

After the two had talked for some time, Ann dozed off again. Margaret eased out of the room.

When the doctor came to the nurse's station, Margaret asked him, "How much time does Ann Mitchell have?"

Dr. Thomas looked over her chart and said, "She's in her last stages. No more than six months. I'm surprised that she's held on this long."

* * *

When Margaret went home, she heated up the food her housekeeper had cooked. As she sat down to eat, she thought about what the doctor said. Margaret's heart was so heavy she couldn't eat. She wrapped her food up and put it in the refrigerator, then went upstairs and looked in on Ana. She kissed her baby and fixed her covers. Margaret went into her room, took a quick shower, and lay down. She lay there for hours unable to sleep, thinking about what the doctor told her about Ann. She thought about her adopted mother's last words. Margaret got out of bed and went through photos that her adoptive mother had left.

There was one in particular of Margaret and her biological mother. She stared at the picture and thought about how beautiful her mother. Then she thought about Ana. Margaret couldn't conceive how a mother could give her child up. She tried to put herself in Ann's shoes. She thought about how difficult it had been for her to do all that she did and then make it out. She wondered if Ann would have had an easier or different life if her mother had chosen to give her up.

Although Margaret had a decent childhood, she still longed for her biological mother. Margaret's adoptive mother told her on her eighteenth birthday that she was adopted. Margaret thought back. She could still remember that day. She woke up, excited that she was now eighteen. She was an adult, in her second year of college. It was a Friday, and she and a few friends were going out that night. That afternoon, when she got home from her classes, her adoptive mother Mary was sitting in the living room. This surprised Margaret because Mary was normally working at that time.

Mary said, "Come in here, baby."

Margaret obeyed. "What is it, Mom?"

"Baby, sit down."

"Mom, come on. I have to get ready for tonight."

"Baby, I have something to tell you. I figured you're grown now, you can handle it."

"What's wrong?"

"Baby, sit next to me." Mary took Margaret's hands in hers. "Baby, I know it's your birthday. I don't mean to spoil it, but I'm running out of time." Margaret was starting to get worried. Mary continued, "Baby I don't have much time to live. I have ovarian cancer. They say there's nothing that they can do. I opted not to take treatment because it won't cure me. It would just prolong the inevitable and I won't be able to do what I need to get ready. Baby, I went to an attorney this morning; everything that I own has been transferred over into your name. You are to finish school. Your loans will be paid upon my death."

Margaret began to cry.

"Listen up." Mary picked up a folder and handed it to Margaret. "In this folder is everything you need. Tomorrow we need to go to the bank so I can put your name on my accounts so you won't have a problem getting money. Everything has been taken care of for my burial. I've talked to the minister about the program. It's done, and he'll be here for you. Everything has been paid for, so all the policies are yours. I'm sorry to tell you on your birthday, but there's no more time. Baby, there's one other thing." Mary put her arm around Margaret. "Baby, I'm not your biological mother. I adopted you when you were one. Your mother couldn't keep you. She was young and didn't have any support. I'm telling you this because I don't want you to be alone." Mary took a piece of paper out of her pocket and gave it to Margaret. "The last information I have is that she and her husband live here. This is their number and address."

Margaret trembled as she cried. She didn't know what to say. She couldn't believe what she was hearing.

Mary held her and said, "I know this is a lot to deal with. I didn't know when to tell you, but time is not on our side. Understand, I was going to the doctor, but they didn't pick it up. By the time they found it, the cancer had already spread. Baby, I want you to go out and celebrate your birthday. You only get one eighteenth birthday."

Margaret went up to her room and cried. Awhile later, her phone rang, and she picked it up.

"Hello."

"Hi! Happy birthday. Are you almost ready?"

"I will be by the time you get here."

"Okay. See you soon."

When her friend Sharon came over, Margaret put on a brave face. She kissed and hugged Mary.

Mary called behind her, "Have a good time!"

Margaret and Sharon went over to a nightclub in New York. Sharon tried to get Margaret to drink, but Margaret couldn't imagine drinking because she was already numb. Sharon asked her what was wrong, but Margaret told her nothing. The two left before the club closed, and then Sharon dropped Margaret off.

For the next month, Margaret stayed close to home. She kept tabs on Mary. By the end of the second month, Mary had to leave work because she was in too much pain. By the end of the third month, Mary was heavily medicated. Mary died the first week of the fourth month. The funeral was held, and the church took care of the arrangements as had been planned. The minister offered assistance to Margaret, but she declined it. She decided to face the world alone.

* * *

Margaret thought about the envelope that Mary had given her on her eighteenth birthday. She got it out of the cabinet and looked through it. It had a letter and a picture. She reread the letter.

Hi, Baby Girl,

If you're reading this, my wished was carried out. I got to meet your new mom. She seems to be a good person, and I hope she will love you as much as I do.

Baby, don't ever think that I gave you up because I didn't love you; it's quite the opposite. I gave you up because I love you.

Baby, I gave you up because I didn't want you to live the way I did, and I don't want to do to you what my mother did to me.

I want you to have more happy days than sad. I want you to have—if there is such a thing—as normal a life as possible, with friends, boyfriends, college, proms, and graduations.

I wrote you this letter because I want you to know that your mommy loved you with all of my heart, and I hope that you forgive me.

Maybe one day when you're all grown up you'll get to show me that I was right by letting you have the life that all little girls should have.

I love you,
Mommy

Tears came into Margaret's eyes. She remembered that on the day before Mary died, through a strained voice of pain and medication, she said, "I love you, Margaret, as if I gave birth to you. You are my daughter. Don't be too sad. Just think, you have two mothers who love you very much."

Margaret climbed back into bed and drifted off to sleep. When morning came, Margaret got up reluctantly. She was tired and bewildered about telling her mother who she was. Margaret went into Ana's room. Ana was still asleep, so Margaret went to take a shower. She just stood as the warm water flowed over her body. After ten minutes, Margaret began to wash herself. When she got out of the shower, Ana had awakened and was calling for her. Margaret hastily dried herself and then went into Ana's room.

"Hi, baby."

"Good morning. I was calling you."

Margaret leaned over her daughter, picked her up, and hugged her. "I know. Mommy was taking a shower."

"Where are you going?"

"Nowhere, baby."

"You're off?"

"Yes. Are you hungry?"

"Yes. Can I help cook?"

"Yes. What would you like?"

"Pannie cakes and bacon."

"Anything else?"

"Eggs."

"Okay. Let's go."

Margaret carried Ana down to the kitchen.

As they were fixing breakfast, Ana asked, "Mommy, was that Grand-mom?"

"Who, baby?"

"The sick lady."

"Why would you think that?"

"She looks like Grand-mom."

Margaret became curious. "How do you know what Grand-mom looks like?"

"I don't know. Where's daddy?"

"I guess he's home."

"When is he coming to get me?"

"I don't know baby. Your father is very busy."

Ana looked sad. She asked, "Are you very busy?"

"Never for you, baby." She kissed Ana on her forehead.

While they were eating, Ana said, "Mommy, are we going to visit that sick lady today?"

"Would you like to?"

"Yes."

"Okay, let's get dressed."

Ana jumped up.

Margaret dressed Ana and then put her in her car seat and drove to the hospital. When they arrived at the hospital, the doctors and nurses were running to Ann's room. Margaret picked Ana up.

Ana said, "What's going on, Mommy?"

Margaret didn't respond. Ana wrapped her arms around her mother's neck. Awhile later, the staff came out of Ann's room, and Dr. Thomas said, "That was close."

Margaret asked, "Can we go in?"

"Yes. But let her rest."

Margaret walked into the room. Ann was sleeping. Margaret sat frozen for an hour, and Ana continued to hold on to her mother. She did not make a sound. After an hour, Margaret touched Ann's hand, then left.

That night, Margaret had a restless sleep. She was off again the next day but decided to get the housekeeper to come in to watch Ana so that she could go to the hospital. When the housekeeper arrived, Margaret left for the hospital.

When she went into Ann's room, she was happy to see that Ann was awake and alert.

Ann said, "Hi, baby. How are you today?"

"I'm better that you're still here."

"Thank you, baby. That's nice of you. I heard I gave them a run for their money."

"Yes you did."

"Margaret, I need you to make sure that next time they let me go. You understand what I'm saying?"

"Yes."

"Can you do that for me?"

"Yes."

"Promise. I've been here long enough without Mark."

"I promise, but do you know that there are other people here?"

"I know, but I'm tired. If I can't stay here without the machine's help, it's time for me to leave."

"Ann, there's something I need to tell you."

"What is it, baby?"

"It's hard … I don't know how to say it."

31

"It's only as hard as you make it. Is it something that will do harm?"

"I don't think so."

Just then, the on-duty nurse came in and took Ann's vitals. After she was done, Ann drifted off to sleep. Margaret stayed a little while longer, but it appeared that Ann needed rest.

The rest of the week, Ann was in and out of consciousness.

The next week, Margaret seemed to be somewhere else; she made her rounds but did so mechanically. On Friday, Margaret was happy that she had the weekend off. At the end of her shift, as always she went to check on Ann. Ann was alert.

Ann said, "Hi, baby. How are you today?"

"I'm fine."

"You look like you're troubled about something."

"Kind of."

"Weren't we supposed to discuss something? I forget when, but we started a conversation."

"Yes."

"Well what was it that you wanted to say?"

"It's hard."

"Baby, if something is bothering you to the point you're walking around like you have for over a week, you need to just say it."

Margaret sat down. Then she got up. "I'll be right back. I have to get something."

Margaret went to her locker, retrieved an envelope, and then returned to Ann's room.

Margaret handed Ann the envelope.

Ann said, "What's this?"

"Look in it."

Ann opened the envelope. She pulled out a letter, then a picture. She looked at the photo. Ann smiled.

Margaret said, "Look familiar?"

Ann said, "That's me. I was pretty then."

"You're still nice looking."

"Thank you, baby, but it's been a long time since I was this good looking."

Ann unfolded the letter and read it.

After she read it, Margaret said, "Does that look familiar too?"

Ann looked up with tear-filled eyes. For fifteen minutes, neither woman spoke.

It was Ann who broke the silence. "I always thought that you were my baby, but I wasn't positive. You mean that precious baby is my granddaughter? Come here, baby."

Margaret got up, walked over to Ann's bed, and bent down. Ann put her arms around Margaret, and they both cried.

Through tears and a shaky voice, Ann said, "I hoped that you were my baby. I waited so long for you to come. I heard Mary passed awhile ago. I'm sorry I couldn't be there for you. When I found out, I wanted to be there for you, but Mark reminded me that Mary may not have told you about me. Many nights, he held me while I cried. I felt so helpless. I didn't want to enter your world and turn it upside down, so I waited. I thought I was going to have to leave this world without seeing you grown up. Mark used to try to reassure me that I would. And here you are."

"My mother, Mary, told me when I was eighteen, but I shut down."

"That's all right. We're here now."

"I wasted so much time."

"We have now; that's all that matters. Tell me about your childhood. Were you a good girl, or did you get into a lot of trouble?"

"I was good. I just had a bit of a mouth."

"Just like your grandmother. On good days, she would tell me about her childhood. She said that she would give her mother word for word. She got a lot of whippings. Baby, look down in that drawer." Margaret opened the drawer Ann was pointing to. "Get my purse. Take my keys out of it. I want you to go to my house. Go up to my bedroom—you'll know which one it is. I have a box on my side of the bed. It has all my important documents in it. In the nightstand near it are all my photo albums. Get them for me and bring them to the hospital when you're back on duty."

"I'll bring them tomorrow."

"Are you sure?"

"Yes. I've wasted too much time."

"Baby, give me my wallet."

Margaret gave Ann the wallet. Ann shakily opened her wallet and took out a business card. She handed it to Margaret.

"Tomorrow, call this number and ask for Thomas. Tell him I asked you to call. Tell him I need him to come see me."

* * *

The next day, Margaret got up early. She dressed Ana, and they headed to Ann's house. It was a house big enough for a growing family to be comfortable in, elegantly furnished and neatly kept. It appeared that someone was keeping it dusted. Margaret went upstairs. She glanced in the first bedroom. It looked like a guestroom. The bedroom across the hall also looked like a guestroom. As she continued down the hall, she passed a full bathroom that was large and had an old-fashioned tub that. A little further down the hall, on the opposite side was a small room.

It looked like it was used as a sitting room.

She finally made it to the back of the house. The master bedroom suite was the size of two large rooms and was decorated in an old French style. There was a large sitting area, and Margaret could tell that Ann had spent much of her time there when she was in her bedroom. Not that it was worn-looking; it was simply intimate in its nature with the loveseat and chaise. There was a handmade shawl draped over the back of the loveseat and papers that were of a personal nature on it. The other side of the room had a king-size bed with a high post and sheer drapes. Margaret knew which side of the bed was Mark's because it still had his slippers neatly kept. They were positioned for him when he would get out of the bed. On the other side of the bed was the box Ann had spoken of. Margaret didn't open it. She looked in the nightstand. It held six albums. Margaret put them on top of the box and picked them up. She told Ana to hold on to the banister.

When they got to the hospital, Margaret instructed Ana to hold on to her jacket. They entered the hospital and went to Ann's room.

Ana said, "She's asleep, Mommy."

"I know. We'll just sit here quietly until she wakes up."

"Okay, Mommy."

Just then, Ann woke up. She focused her eyes, smiled, and said, "Hi."

Margaret smiled and then turned to her daughter and said, "Ana, I would like to introduce you to your grand-mom."

"I know," Ana said.

"What do you know?"

"My grand-mom."

"How did you know?"

Ana shrugged her shoulders and then walked over to Ann. Margaret lifted her up so could see Ann better. Ana reached over to hug Ann, and as they hugged, Ana said, "I love you, Grand-mom."

Ann kissed Ana and said, "I love you too, baby."

Concerned about Ann's strength, Margaret said, "Okay, Ana." She picked Ana up and sat her in a chair and then said, "Ann—I mean, Mom …"

"Baby, call me what you're comfortable with. Don't force yourself to say anything that you're not feeling."

"Ann, I brought everything you asked for."

Ann sat up, and Margaret helped her to get comfortable.

"Put the box over there" Ann said, pointing to the clothes closet. "Hand me the albums, and come closer."

They spent the afternoon looking through the photos. They were pictures that were left by Ann's mother. Ann told her who all the people were. By the third album, Margaret felt as though she knew everyone in the photos. The fourth album had a lot of pictures of Ann from when she was a baby up to early adulthood. It had also had pictures of Ann's mother in it.

Ann said, "This is your grandmother. Wasn't she beautiful?"

Margaret studied the picture. She tried to imagine what her grandmother sounded like, her walk, and even her mannerisms.

Margaret said, "Yes, she was very beautiful."

"You know, you look like her."

"Do you think? I think she was better looking."

"You look like her. You could be her twin." Ann showed her several other pictures towards the back of the album and then said, "Who's this?"

Margaret looked.

Ann continued, "This is you in the hospital when you were first born. These are more pictures of you." Pointing to the pictures, Ann said to Ana, "This is your mommy."

Ann took a photo out of the book and handed it to Margaret, saying, "Read the back."

Tears formed in Margaret's eyes. She said, "You named me?"

"Yes, after your grandmother. Her name was Margaret Ann."

Margaret stared at the picture. She didn't speak. Then she returned the picture to the album, and they moved on to the fifth album.

In the fifth album was a dedication about the love that Mark and Ann felt for each other. Margaret said, "He was very handsome."

"Wasn't he? Sometimes I would lay and watch him sleep. You know, he was good at everything he did. We used to go out dancing. He knew all the latest dances. He even knew many formal dances. He loved to dance." Ann ran her hand over his picture.

Margaret said, "I would have liked to have known him."

Ann said, "Me too—I wish you could have met him."

Margaret saw that Ann was getting tired and said, "Well it's getting late. I need to get Ana home."

"Okay."

"I'll come back tomorrow."

"Okay, baby."

Ann laid her head back.

Ana said, "I want to kiss Grand-mom bye."

Margaret picked Ana up, and Ana kissed and hugged Ann.

Ann said, "Goodnight, baby."

* * *

That night, Margaret lay in bed unable to sleep. Her mind played back the photos that she had seen earlier. She smiled as she remembered the stories that Ann told her. Margaret wrapped her arms around herself thinking of Ann's hug. She cried herself to sleep as she thought of all that she missed and all the time she would never have with her mother.

The next morning, she woke up early and got Ana dressed.

Ana said, "We going to church, Mommy?"

"Kind of. We'll go to see Grand-mom and watch church on her TV."

After getting dressed, they headed to the hospital. When they got there, Ann was awake and eating. Margaret and Ana kissed Ann on the cheek.

Ann said, "Good morning. Where are you two going today?"

"We figured we'd come go to church with you."

Ann looked puzzled.

"On TV," Margaret said.

Ann smiled and turned the TV to channel five.

When the program ended, Ann said, "Isn't it something how sometimes it seems like they're talking to you?"

"Yes it does. It did seem like he was talking to us. How are you feeling today?"

"I'm feeling much better this morning."

"That's good."

They spent all of the morning and early afternoon catching up on each other's lives. By two o'clock, Ana was getting fidgety, so Margaret decided to leave.

* * *

On Monday morning, Thomas came to visit Ann.

He said, "How are you, Ann?"

"I'm much better than I've been."

"That's good. What brought on the change?"

"My daughter. Yes, I have a daughter and as a matter of fact a granddaughter."

"When did all of this happen?"

"Oh about twenty-three years ago."

"You never told me you had a daughter."

41

"That's because I gave her away." Thomas looked at her bewildered. "When I was very young, I got pregnant. I didn't have any support, and I was alone. I wanted to give my daughter a chance in life. So when she was one, I gave her up for adoption. I wrote her a letter and put my picture in the envelope with it."

"How do you know that this woman is your daughter? Maybe she found your letter."

"No. I gave it to the woman who adopted her. So she had to give it to her."

"Maybe the woman is trying to scam you," Thomas cautioned her.

"No. The woman has since died. Besides, she looks just like my mother. She's my daughter. That's why I called for you to come here. I need to update my will. I also need you to change ownership of my property to my daughter."

"Ann, are you sure you want to do this so soon?"

"Thomas, I've run out of time. I'm not a sick woman who is desperate to take anyone in. I'm positive this woman is my child. Besides, there's no one for the money to go to anyway. I'm leaving everything to my daughter, except $100,000. I want it to go in a trust fund for my granddaughter. Change all of my stock and bonds to my daughter's name immediately. I don't want her having any problems getting the money. By the way, have you found anyone yet?"

"No."

"Are you dating anyone?"

"No. Why?"

"I was just asking. You're a nice young man. From what I see, you'd make a woman a good husband."

"Don't start trying to fix me up with anyone."

"I'm not."

"Okay. I'll get these things taken care of, and I'll come back next week for you to sign off on the papers."

"Thank you, Thomas."

Thomas had known Ann and had done business with her since he earned his law degree. He felt compelled to make sure she wasn't being taken advantage of. He decided to run a background check on Margaret. When her record came back clean, he decided to investigate further. What he found eased his mind about completing the task that had been given to him by Ann.

When the following Monday came, Thomas brought the documents for Ann to sign. Ann instructed him to hand over the file to Margaret upon her death.

While he was still there, Margaret entered Ann's room. She was on duty. Before she saw Thomas, Margaret said, "Hi, Ann. How are you today?"

Ann said, "Hi. Margaret." Just then, Margaret noticed Thomas. "Margaret, this is Thomas."

Thomas looked up. He was mesmerized by Margaret's large, dark brown eyes that slanted in the corner.

By the time Ann said, "Thomas this is my daughter," he was already standing up. They shook hands and said hello to each other.

Ann said, "Margaret, Thomas is my attorney and a long-time good friend."

Thomas said, "I've heard a lot about you."

Margaret said, "Really?" She looked at Ann.

Ann smiled and said, "Actually, I just told him that I had found my daughter. He's just realizing that you're a nurse here and how beautiful you are."

Margaret blushed. "Mom, stop!"

Ann looked at her in surprise. It was the second time that Margaret had called her mom. The first time was merely out of obligation. This time was different. She felt that Margaret meant to call her this, because she had formed a bond.

Margaret went on, "I came in to check on you and take your vitals. I didn't know you had company. I can come back."

Thomas said, "No ... don't let me stop you from doing your job."

Margaret looked at Ann and said, "Do you mind?"

"No, baby."

While Margaret was performing her tasks, she could feel Thomas watching her. She was flattered and held back a smile.

Thomas turned his attention to Ann, resuming their conversation. Margaret took the opportunity to get a better look at his well-built body and perfect posture, as well as his short hair and well-sculpted sideburns, mustache, and goatee. He looked over and caught her checking him out and smiled. Margaret excused herself and left the room.

Ann said, "Thomas isn't my daughter beautiful?"

"Yes she is. You never mentioned that."

"Well she's my daughter, so I'm a little biased. Are you interested in getting to know her?"

"Why are you always trying to fix me up?"

"Because you need companionship. Thomas, you're such a nice guy, I just think that any woman who gets you would be lucky—and I'm not talking financially."

"Thank you for your confidence. I'm attracted to your daughter, but you two just found each other. I don't want to impose and take away from the time you have together."

"Well I won't harass you about it. What's meant to be will be."

"Ann, it has been a pleasure, but I must go." Thomas bent down and kissed her on her forehead.

"Okay. Don't be a stranger."

"I'll get back out soon."

Thomas left the room, and as he was walking down the hall, Margaret was coming out of a patient's room. He saw her and stopped.

"Excuse me, Margaret, can I speak to you for a second?" he said.

"Sure, come in here." Thomas followed her into an empty room. "What can I do for you?"

"I need to ask you a personal question."

"What is it?'

"How is Ann doing? I mean does she have much time?"

Sadness came over Margaret's face, and Thomas wanted to take her in his arms to comfort her.

Margaret answered, "I talked to the doctor. He doesn't think she'll be here much longer. We almost lost her a few weeks ago. I don't know if she told you, but that's why I finally told her who I was. Before she knew who I was, she was so nice to me and really opened up. I didn't want her to leave this world without knowing me."

"I understand," Thomas said. "She's been like a mother to me. When I met her, I was finishing school—I was interning. I had to prepare legal papers when her husband got sick."

"Did you know her husband?"

"Yes. Mark was an extraordinary man. The love that those two exhibited was remarkable. I went to the funeral. She held up better than I thought she would have, but I felt bad for her because she was all alone."

"I wish I could have been there for her. But I was going through some stuff myself."

"I'm sorry to hear that," Thomas said.

"No. I'm fine now. It just shook me when I found out that I was adopted. My adoptive mother told me on my eighteenth birthday that she was dying from cancer and that I was adopted. I understand now that she wanted me to have someone, but I didn't take it well. I shut down. It took me all these years to deal with this. It feels like God *wanted* me to deal with this. I mean, how ironic is it that my mother would end up in the hospital that I work in."

"I'm glad that she has someone with her during her last days. I'm sorry, I'm keeping you. I was concerned about her and would like to spend as much time with her as I can before she goes."

"That's nice. From the way she spoke of you, I'm sure she'll enjoy that. But you're wrong about keeping me from anything; I'm actually off."

Thomas surprised himself by asking Margaret, "If you have some time, would you like to go somewhere and have a cup of tea?"

"Let me sign out and say bye to my mother. I'll be right back."

Margaret signed out at the nurse's station and went into Ann's room. "Mom, I'm leaving now. I'll see you tomorrow."

"Okay, baby."

Margaret kissed and hugged Ann and then went back to where she had left Thomas.

As they left the hospital, Margaret said, "There's an IHOP down the street, or we could go a little further down the other way where there are a few other restaurants."

"IHOP is fine."

As they walked, Thomas said, "So are you married or dating anyone?" He couldn't believe he had been so blunt.

She smiled and said, "No, on both."

"Oh. I didn't mean to sound liked I was coming on to you."

"No harm done." Changing the subject, she said, "So you've known Ann for a long time?"

"For about five years. She came to my firm when Mark got sick. For some reason, they took a liking to me. After a couple of times of meeting with them while preparing their paperwork, they invited me to dinner.

After that, I became a regular for Sunday dinner. They treated me like a son."

"I don't know if either of them ever told you that they wanted children, but after me, my mother wasn't able to carry any children to full term."

"No, I didn't know that. I use to wonder if they had any children and where they were."

"I guess you fit what they would have liked if they had been able to have a son. Can I ask you a personal question?" Margaret said.

"Shoot."

"Where are your parents?"

"My mother died of breast cancer five years ago, and my father died a year to the date. Some say it was heartbreak; others blame it on him not taking care of himself when my mother got sick. I think it was a combination of both. She did everything for him. When she got sick, he didn't watch his diet. He already had a heart condition. He had a severe heart attack. He had previously made a living will of no resuscitation. He didn't want to live without my mother. The night he died, he had a peaceful look on his face."

"I didn't mean to bring up bad memories."

"You didn't," Thomas assured her. "I had a good relationship with my parents, and I've made peace with it all. I know it might sound strange, but they had each other before they had me. Children move on to their own lives, and unless parents have someone else in their lives, they're virtually alone."

"That's an interesting way to think about it. I was angry at my adoptive mother for telling me on what I thought was supposed to be my big day. I was becoming a woman. Then I was upset with her for leaving me. Then I was angry because she kept it from me, and finally I was angry at my real mother because she gave me away."

"Didn't your adoptive mother tell you why?"

"Yes, but at eighteen years old, I didn't understand why it had to happen to me and why I had to find out on that day. She died three months later. I poured myself into school and graduated at the top of my class, magnum cum laude. I promised Mary, my adoptive mother, that I would finish school. In a weird way, I had it in my mind that I was going to show the world that I didn't need anyone. For a while, I was fine. But on graduation day, when I was getting my master's, I looked out into the audience and realized I was all alone. I cried that night. That's when I changed. I was no longer angry, but I still couldn't bring myself to reach out to my mother."

Thomas glanced at the clock on the wall. He said, "Wow, it's late. I didn't mean to take up this much of your time."

"I didn't realize I had talked that long."

"I think I better let you go. I'm sure you have more pressing things to do than sit here with me."

"It's been nice," Margaret said. "I don't usually talk to strangers this much. I feel comfortable talking with you."

"I'm happy to hear that. I don't like to talk on the phone; I like to see people face-to-face when we talk. Would you—that's if you don't have any plans—would you have lunch with me tomorrow?"

"I plan to visit my mother tomorrow, but if you don't mind a late lunch, I can be available at about three."

"That will be fine. Where would you like to meet?"

"Where are we going to have lunch?"

"Are you familiar with Route 22?"

"Yes."

"On the east side, there's a Spanish restaurant, right after the movies going west."

"I know where that is. We can meet there."

Thomas got up and put his hand out to help Margaret up. She took it, and then he quickly released it. As he opened the door, he put his hand around her waist and she walked out the door with him following. He put his hands behind his back as they walked back to the hospital.

When they got to the parking garage, he waited until Margaret got into her car. She rolled her window down, and he put his hands on her car door. Thomas said, "It has been a pleasure, Miss Daniels." He tapped the car and walked away.

As Margaret drove away, she thought about her conversation with Thomas. It dawned on her that he used her last name, but she hadn't told him what it was. This concerned her.

* * *

The next day, Margaret got up early, dressed Ana, and they went to see Ann. During their visit, Ana fell asleep, and Margaret told Ann about her time with Thomas the day before and her date for lunch. Ann was thrilled.

Margaret asked, "Mom, did you give Thomas my last name?"

Ann didn't remember her business with Thomas.

After visiting with her mother, Margaret dropped Ana at the sitters and headed to the restaurant. When she arrived at the restaurant, Thomas was not there. She gave her name, but they did not have her name in their reservation book. She pulled out Thomas's business card. She gave his name, and they seated her at a table in a dimly lit corner. There was a bouquet of lilies and a card attached. Margaret opened the card. It said: *Look behind you.* She looked, and Thomas was there. He smiled, bent down, kissed her on the cheek, and then sat down.

"Hi," Thomas said.

"Hi. The flowers are beautiful."

"Just like you."

After ordering the food, Thomas asked, "How is Ann today?"

"She's as good as can be expected. Speaking of my mother, how did you know my last name?"

"I was doing some paperwork for your mother. I have to tell you, I conducted a background check on you. I did it to make sure you weren't trying to scam Ann."

Margaret was speechless.

Thomas continued, "Don't get angry. It was before I met you. I was looking out for Ann. I care about her, and it's my job as her attorney and a friend to look out for her."

Margaret thought about it for a moment and then said, "I forgive you."

"Thank you."

After the food came, they ate.

Thomas said, "Margaret, I would like to spend some time with you, to get to know you better."

Margaret began, "I would like that too. I didn't ask you yesterday because I didn't want to seem forward or desperate."

Thomas said, "I'm single. I've never been married. I've never even been close to marriage. Not because I'm afraid of commitment. I always kept my focus on my career. I don't have any children."

Margaret contemplated whether she should tell Thomas about Ana. She said, "Thomas there's something that I have to tell you that might change your mind about me."

"What's that?"

"I have a child. A little girl. She's three years old."

"Okay."

"Okay?"

"Yes. What did you expect me to say?"

"I don't know. I expected more emotion."

"Margaret, I really like you, and I've never run from responsibility. What about the father?"

"It didn't work out. He's in her life. Financially, he's great, but he doesn't always visit."

"Were you in love?"

"I thought I was, but looking back, I think I needed someone to love. When I met him, I was still empty. At the time, I thought that he filled that hole. After I got pregnant, something changed. I think he felt trapped. After I had my baby, we sat down and mapped out how he would provide for her."

"Do you communicate much?"

"No. He sends the payments, and he occasionally calls to speak to his daughter."

"Have you ever thought of having any more children?" Thomas asked.

"I haven't thought about it, but if the right man came along and we got married, I suppose I would be willing to. What about you? Do you want to get married?"

"One day."

Margaret thought, *Is this man for real, or is he just good at being convincing? He is a lawyer after all.*

Thomas said, "I know what you're thinking. You're thinking that I'm running a line. Margaret, you are absolutely beautiful. You have a tight conversation, and I like that you're open. Right now I would like to get to know you, and wherever it leads to, I'm willing to go."

"That sounds fair."

"Can I have your number?"

Teasingly, Margaret said, "I thought you don't like to talk on the phone."

"There will be occasions I would like to call you for a date."

Margaret gave him her cell phone number.

"Well, I've kept you long enough. You have a little girl to go home to. I won't keep you. I'll call you."

They got up from the table, and Thomas took the vase of flowers and handed them to Margaret. He put his hand behind her back and escorted her to her car and then lightly kissed her on the check.

Several days went by before Margaret heard from Thomas. She had come home late from seeing Ann, and when she walked in the door, the phone rang.

Margaret said, "Hello."

Thomas said, "Hi, beautiful."

"Hi, Thomas."

"Are you okay?"

"It's been rough."

"What happened?"

"My mother was touch and go. A few times, we thought we had lost her."

"Do you mind if I go to see her?"

"You don't have to ask. I know she would love to see you."

"Margaret," Thomas said, "you can always call me if you need someone to talk to."

"I'll keep that in mind."

The next day, Margaret went to work. After completing her rounds, she went to spend the rest of the afternoon with Ann.

Margaret entered Ann's room and said, "Hi, Mom."

Ann opened her eyes. "Hi, baby."

"How are you doing?"

"I was dreaming. Mark and I were walking. He held my hand, and I asked him where we were going. He told me that it was a surprise. As we were walking, I saw a cabin ahead of us. When we got closer, I looked down and saw that Mark was no longer holding my hand. When I looked up, he was further ahead of me. I tried to walk faster, but he and the cabin were getting further away. Then they disappeared. Then the dream changed, and I was in my house. I was sitting on my side of the bed. Mark was on his. I asked him why he keeps leaving me. He said that I wasn't ready to be with him. That I wasn't finished here."

Thomas walked in the room just then. He kissed Ann on the cheek and casually spoke to Margaret. He didn't know if she wanted her mother to know they'd been hanging out. Margaret shifted her body. Ann noticed.

Ann smiled and said, "I hear you two have been out—twice."

Thomas looked at Margaret and said, "Yes. It was very nice."

Ann could see Margaret's body relax. She said, "I'm glad you two are hitting it off. I knew you would.

Thomas asked, "So how are you doing today, Ann?"

"I'm okay, just missing Mark. I was telling Margaret that I had a dream about him last night."

"I sometimes think about how close you two were," Thomas said.

"We were soul mates."

"See that's what I mean. How did you know?" he asked.

"You just know. When I first meet him, I liked him right off. When I wasn't with him, I would think about him. When I say think, it wasn't just thinking, it was a feeling. It's hard to describe. I just loved him so much."

Margaret said, "I wish I had known him. It seems like you had a beautiful romance."

"Isn't that amazing?" Ann said. "God blessed me with such a wonderful man. You know, I loved the way he smelled. Even after he died, whenever someone would walk past and I'd smell the cologne that he used to wear, I would think of him."

Around 7:30, Ann dozed off. Margaret and Thomas both kissed her on the forehead and then left.

Once they were out of the room, Thomas asked, "Do you have any plans tonight?"

"Actually, I'm free tonight. My daughter's father picked her up for the weekend."

"Really?"

"Yes, it's the first time in six months."

"Would you like to go out somewhere?"

"I need to first go home and change."

"That's fine. Would you like me to pick you up, or would you like to meet me?"

"You can pick me up. How about 9:00?"

"That's fine. Where are we going?"

"There's a comedy club in Newark. They have some good talent."

"I heard about that club. I've thought of going there but never have."

After Margaret gave him her address, and he walked her to her car, they went their separate ways.

Once Margaret was home, she quickly took a shower. Then she looked in her closet and pulled out several outfits. She wanted to look sexy but didn't want to be overly dressed. She decided on a wraparound dress that showed off her curves but wasn't too revealing. She picked out a pair of heels with a matching purse and then chose a choker and earrings to match. When she was dressed, she gave herself a once-over look. She took out her lightweight leather jacket because it had gotten a little chilly outside.

At nine o'clock, Margaret's doorbell rang. She went down to answer it. When she opened the door, she was taken aback at how breathtaking Thomas looked. He smiled and then bent over and kissed her on the cheek.

He said, "Are you ready?"

"Yes."

He took her arm, led her to his car, and then helped her in.

Thomas drove to the club where they enjoyed the show for the next two hours. In between acts, they talked about the comedians. After the show was over, Thomas drove Margaret home.

When they arrived at her house, Thomas said, "I hate for this date to end."

Margaret said, "It doesn't have to. My daughter isn't home; you can come in, and we can sit and talk."

"Are you sure?'

"Yes."

Thomas got out of the car, walked over to the passenger's side, and opened the door for her. He held out his hand. Margaret took it, and he helped her out of the car. They walked up the stairs hand in hand. Margaret opened her front door.

She led him to the living room and said, "Would you like something to drink?"

"What do you have?"

"I haven't had company in some time, so I only have apple juice, grape juice, cranberry juice, and water."

"I'll take water."

"Let me take your jacket."

He took off his jacket and gave it to her. She hung it up and then took her jacket off and hung it up. Margaret went into the kitchen, retrieved two bottles of water, and returned to the living room. She handed the water to him.

"Thank you."

"You're welcome."

Margaret set next to him and took off her shoes.

"I meant to tell you that you look beautiful," Thomas said.

"Thank you."

"Did you have a good time tonight?"

"Yes. How about you?"

"I always have a good time when I'm with you. Margaret, what made you ask me in?"

"My mother likes you. She respects you. I figured if she could trust you, I would try."

"That's the only reason?"

"No. I feel comfortable with you. I feel like I've known you for a while."

"I feel the same way. I thought it was just me. Is it too soon, or should we make this exclusive?"

"You want to date me?" Margaret asked.

"I've wanted to date you from the first day I met you. Do you think I'm moving too fast?"

"No," she said.

"So?"

"Yes."

"Now that we've gotten that out of the way, when is the last time you've been out with a man?"

"Two and a half years."

"Really?"

"Yes. I tried to make it work with my daughter's father, but nothing I did changed anything. He wanted us to move in together. He said that we could try that out first and see if that worked. I declined the offer. I felt if he was going to marry me, he would do it without us having to live together. I also thought that it would be a waste of time. I didn't feel like he was being sincere. I know that I should have waited to have sex too, but at the time I needed someone in my life."

"Do you ever miss him?"

"I never missed him. He was the first man that I let get that close. When we parted, it was almost a relief. I can't explain it. I take care of my daughter. I go to work. Before my mother came into my life—I mean, came into the hospital and I realized it was her—I never thought of anything other than raising my daughter. What about you? When was the last time you were out on a date?"

"I've taken women out. Nothing ever manifested with any of them. I just didn't feel they were real. I haven't dated anyone in five years. No, I haven't been in love. There was one woman. She was someone that I knew from childhood. We met up in college and again months after we graduated. It was like an off-and-on type of thing. She was into her career as much as I was into mine."

After some time, they got quiet. Thomas took her hands in his.

He asked, "May I kiss you?"

Margaret looked into his eyes. He moved closer to her. While continuing to hold one hand, he placed his other hand under her chin and pulled her to him. He gently kissed her on the lips. He released her hand and put it around her waist pulling her closer to him. As he felt himself becoming aroused, he pulled back. He looked into her eyes and saw desire. He pulled her closer and leaned back on the coach. He just held her. Both were quiet, not wanting to end what they were feeling. He closed his eyes, and Margaret laid her head on his chest. They both drifted off to sleep.

They awakened at five in the morning.

Thomas said, "Hi, beautiful." Margaret smiled. "I think I should go home. Do you have to work?"

"No. I'm off this weekend."

"I know you want to spend time with your mother, but after that, would you like to do something with me when you're free?"

"Yes."

"Well I better let you get some rest. Call me when you're available."

"I will."

Thomas stood up, took her by the hand, and they walked to the door. He took her into his arms and kissed her. After a few minutes, he stopped and pulled away.

"I better go."

Margaret smiled and then went into the closet to get his jacket. He took it and put it on. He bent over and kissed her once again. This time it was brief.

"See you, beautiful."

After Thomas left, Margaret went up to her room. She undressed and got into bed. She thought about her night and then drifted off to sleep.

The next morning, Margaret awakened at nine. After showering and getting dressed, she called Ana and talked to her for a few minutes. Ana's father, Steve, then took the phone and let Margaret know he would bring Ana home the next day around five o'clock."

Margaret left for the hospital. When she arrived, she checked in and went into Ann's room. She checked Ann's chart and saw that they had increased Ann's medication. Margaret kissed Ann on the forehead. Ann did not wake up.

When the nurse on duty came in, she said to Margaret. "You're not on duty, are you?"

"No. I'm visiting."

"You visit Mrs. Miller a lot."

"She's my mother."

The nurse looked bewildered.

Margaret went on, "Yes, I just found out."

"I'm sorry."

"Thank you," Margaret said.

"She had a bad night. She was in a lot of pain. She was calling someone name Mark."

"That was her husband. He passed away a few years ago."

"That's so sad. I'll leave you to spend time will Mrs. Miller alone."

"Thank you."

Margaret moved her chair closer to the bed and held Ann's hand. After an hour, Margaret put her head down, resting it near Ann. She fell asleep.

When she awakened, it was three o'clock. She looked at Ann's chart and saw that someone had been in to check the vitals and nothing had changed. She sat there watching her mother breathe. At seven, Thomas walked into the room. He kissed Margaret and then Ann on the forehead. He pulled his chair close to Margaret and placed his hand on hers.

"How is she?" he asked.

"They've increased her pain medication. She's been like this since I got here."

"Have you eaten?"

"No. I'm not hungry."

He pulled her close to him and held her. She leaned against him, still watching Ann. They sat there until Thomas said, "You need to get some rest."

"I don't want to leave her."

"I know, but you have to keep up your strength."

Margaret looked at him and saw genuine concern in his eyes. She got up, kissed her mother, and whispered, "I'll be back tomorrow. I love you." She then went to the nurse's station and asked them to call her if anything changed. They told her they would.

Thomas walked out with her. When they got to her car, Margaret said, "Follow me home." Thomas followed her home. After parking his car, he got out and walked to Margaret's car. He opened the door, held out his hand, and helped her out. He walked her to the door, and she invited him in.

After closing the door, she turned and began to kiss him. Thomas pulled back and looked into Margaret's eyes. What he saw was fear. He walked her into the living room and sat her down. He took her into his arms to comfort her, and she began to cry. He kissed her tears, and she again kissed him, this time with such passion he lost himself in the kiss. They caressed each other. He leaned her back on the couch and then stopped.

Margaret said, "Make love to me."

Thomas sat up, took her face into his hands, and said, "I want to with all of my heart, but I can't right now."

"Why?"

"Because that's not what you need right now. I can make love to you right now to remove you from this moment, but the pain won't go away. I'll be here as much as you want me to be. I'll be here to help you get through this. And I'll comfort you with my strength, but I will not mess up what we have by making love to you before you're ready." He took her into his arms and leaned back on the couch. Soon, they both fell asleep.

When she awakened the next morning at five, she looked up at Thomas and lightly kissed him on the lips. He pulled her to him and kissed her passionately. Her mind whirled. This time, she pulled back. She realized that he was still asleep. As she pulled away, he awakened. He looked at her and then realized where he was. He said, "I'm sorry. I was dreaming about you."

She teased, "What were we doing?"

"I think you know. How are you?"

"I'm better. Thank you."

"I'm glad I could be here for you."

"I'm going up to shower and change so I can go back up to the hospital."

"Okay. I'll let myself out," Thomas said.

"No. Don't' go. Wait for me."

"Are you sure?"

"Yes. Please wait."

While Margaret was upstairs, Thomas fell back asleep on the couch. When Margaret went back downstairs, she lightly kissed him on the lips to wake him up. He opened his eyes and smiled. He pulled her close and kissed her passionately. After a few minutes, he stopped and kissed her on the forehead.

He said, "I think I better leave now."

Outside, Thomas opened her car door for her to get in. After she started the car, he bent down and kissed her on the lips. He asked, "When will I see you again?"

"I don't know. My daughter comes home later today, and I'm not off again until next weekend. I'm working seven days this week."

"We'll work something out. Bye, beautiful."

* * *

When Margaret went into Ann's room, she happy to see her awake and alert.

Margaret said, "Good morning."

"Good morning, baby."

"How are you?"

"I'm okay."

"You scared me," Margaret said.

"How long was I out?"

"You were out all of yesterday. I was worried."

"Baby, you're a strong woman. Don't worry so much. Enjoy the time that we have now. When I'm gone, remember our talks. I wish we could have had more time, but as it stands, we only have what God gives us. Please don't dwell on what we didn't or don't have. How's it going with Thomas?"

"Good."

"Just good? You two are made for each other. I can see it in the way you look at each other."

"How's that?"

"When you look at each other, it's like no one else is in the room."

"I didn't realize it."

"Well you do. I'm happy for the two of you. He needs a good woman in his life. He's a good man. Although he would never admit it, he's lonely."

"What about me?"

"You're not only lonely, but there's something empty inside. You have to learn to accept your past, your present, and embrace your future. Happiness is your future. God has given all of us a second chance. It may not be wrapped the way we would like it, but what we do with the package is what counts."

"I'm going to miss our talks," Margaret said.

"Miss them, treasure them, even embrace them, but don't mourn them."

"How can I not?"

"You have to remember the good things in life. You get down sometimes and that's natural, but you can't stay there. It's not healthy. Look at you. You have a beautiful daughter who adores you. You have a great career and financial support from her father. He may not be there all the time, but at least your daughter knows him and spends some time with him. You had a terrific mom for eighteen years and were given another mother. It may not be the ideal situation, but I'm blessed to have you now. I've always loved you."

"I love you too. I do feel blessed that I have you in my life. I just want you around as long as I live."

"Baby, you have me now. We'd all like our loved ones to be here forever, but God only loans us things. Then we have to give them back. If you believe there is a heaven, we'll all meet up again one day."

Margaret hugged her mother.

At three o'clock, Margaret left the hospital. She wanted to get home just in case Steve dropped Ana off early.

When she arrived home, Margaret straightened up and then cooked dinner. At five, the doorbell rang. She opened the door. Ana was standing there alone. Steve was in the car.

"Hi, Mommy."

"Hi, baby. Say bye to Daddy."

After Ana waived to her father, he drove away.

Margaret and Ana went into the house.

"Did you have a good time with Daddy?"

"Yes."

"What did you do?"

"We went to the zoo with Shirley."

"Who's Shirley?"

"That's daddy's friend. I saw an elephant, a lion, and lots of monkeys."

"Did you like them?"

"Yes. Daddy said we can go back next time."

"Are you hungry?"

"Yes. Shirley doesn't cook."

"What did you eat at Daddy's?"

"McDonalds. I like McDonalds."

"I bet you do. Well let's wash your hands so we can eat."

"Okay."

After washing their hands, they sat down to eat.

Ana said, "Can we visit Grand-mom?"

"Sure. Would you like to go tomorrow?"

"Yes."

That night, Margaret put Ana to bed. While she was reading her a story, Ana said, "Shirley doesn't read stories."

"What does Shirley do?"

"She sleeps. Daddy said I'm going to have a little sister or brother."

"Really? Does Shirley sleep over?"

"Yes. She sleeps with Daddy."

"Is Shirley nice?"

"Yes. She gives me cookies."

Margaret smiled at Ana and kissed her goodnight.

* * *

For the next month, Margaret took Ana to see Ann twice a week. On her days off, Margaret spent much of her time at the hospital. Thomas didn't want to impose, so he called Margaret once a week to check on her. At the end of the month, Thomas called Margaret's cell phone. She was still at work.

She answered, "Hello."

"Hi, beautiful."

"Hi, Thomas. How are you?"

"Better since hearing your voice. Are you home?"

"No. I'm still at work. Why?"

"I was feeling lonely. I would like to spend some time with you. When do you get off?"

"I just clocked out."

"Could we spend some time together tonight?"

"What do you have in mind?"

"I didn't make any arrangements for us to go anywhere. I can come get you and order some takeout and we could have a quiet night together at my house. That's if you don't mind."

"I'll tell you what, to save time, you give me your address, and I'll drive over. Just order the food. I'll make arrangements with the sitter."

"Great. I'll see you soon."

Margaret said good night to her mother and went to her car. Before driving off, she called the housekeeper. When she arrived at Thomas's home, it was seven o'clock. She walked up to the door and rang the bell. Thomas opened the door, took her into his arms, and kissed her. He released her as quickly as he pulled her to him.

"Sorry," he said. "I was just happy to see you."

"Don't be. It's nice to be missed."

"Come in. Are you hungry?"

"A little."

"I didn't know what you wanted to eat, so I ordered several dishes."

He escorted her to the dinning room. Margaret was impressed. He had the dining room lights dim and two candles lit. A bouquet of lilies sat in the middle of the table. There were three different shrimp dishes, lobster tails, and two different vegetable dishes. He held her chair out, and Margaret sat. Once Thomas had sat down, they said their grace privately.

"Everything looks delicious," she said.

"I'm happy you approve."

They passed the food to each other. Margaret tried a little of each dish. During the meal, they caught up on what had been going on in their lives during the past month. After an hour of talking, they moved to the den and sat together in a double chair. Thomas put his arm around her shoulders and showed her family photos. As she looked at them, he caressed her shoulders.

He asked, "How is Ann?"

"She's doing as well as can be expected. She's lasted longer than anyone thought. I think she's stayed this long because of me. I want to let her go, but it's hard."

"I know when my mother was dying, she was in a lot of pain. Although I wanted her pain to go away, I didn't want her to go. I knew that the only way that she was going to be relieved of her pain would be for her to die. You know, it was more painful to watch my father than my mother. You'll find the strength, and what you can't find in yourself, find it in me. I'm here for you."

"Thank you."

Thomas turned Margaret to him. He took his free hand and cupped her face. He said, "You know I missed you?"

She whispered, "Me too."

Thomas looked into her eyes and saw the desire in them. He leaned in and kissed her. She dared not to touch him, trying to keep her control. As he kissed her, he caressed her face. He took both of his hands and pulled her into him, and she wrapped her arms around his neck. They continued to kiss. Thomas picked her up and carried her over to the couch. He sat down with her still in his arms and then leaned back with her. She lay on the inside of the couch next to him. As they kissed, he caressed her body. He pulled her on top of him. He whispered in her ear, "You feel so good." He kissed her neck and behind her ears, sending sparks all over her body. He touched her with such precise gentleness that her body craved more. He stopped briefly and asked, "How much time do we have?"

"All night."

That was the last time they spoke.

The next morning, Margaret awakened at seven. She put her clothes on and went out to her car to get a change of clothes. When she went back into the house, she saw that Thomas had awakened. He was coming out of the den.

"How long have you been up?" he asked.

"Not long."

"Where did you get the clothes?"

"I always keep a change of clothes in my car for when I do doubles."

Thomas smiled. "Let me show you to the bathroom."

She followed him. He turned on the water.

She said, "Care to join me?"

"I'll be back."

She took her clothes off and got into the shower. Just as she began to soap up, Thomas opened the shower door and entered. He took the bath sponge and began to wash Margaret. Then Margaret took the sponge from Thomas and lathered it. She started at his chest, then down his body. He took her hands in his and kissed them. He took her into his arms, lifted her head, and they began to kiss. He stopped kissing her and looked into her eyes.

He said, "I love you, Margaret."

"I love you too."

He took her into his arms and they made love.

Afterwards, as Margaret got dressed, Thomas said, "Do you have to work today?"

"No."

"What are your plans?"

"I'm going to get Ana and visit my mother."

"Ana?" he said.

"I'm sorry. Ana is my daughter. Haven't I spoken of her before?"

"You've spoken of her, but you've never said her name."

"I hadn't realized."

"That's fine. I should let you go; you have a full day."

They kissed good-bye.

* * *

Margaret and Thomas tried to spend as much time together as possible. As the months passed, Ann got weaker, and Margaret spent more time at the hospital. On days when Ann was alert, they would go through the photo albums. Thomas came to visit Ann once a week, first making sure Margaret was not there. Thomas and Ann would reminisce about the past and talk about his relationship with Margaret. On one particular day Thomas went to the hospital, Ann was having a good day.

He said, "Ann, I've come here today to ask your permission."

"Permission for what?"

"I've fallen in love with your daughter. I'm here to ask for her hand in marriage."

"Come here."

Thomas got up and walked over to Ann's bed. She put her arms up. He bent down, and she hugged him.

She said, "Of course, you may marry my daughter. I hope that you'll be as happy as I was and that God will bless you with more time than he granted me and Mark."

"Thank you, Ann."

As he moved away from Ann, Margaret walked into the room. She said, "Hi, Thomas."

He walked over to her and kissed her lightly on the lips.

Thomas said, "I'm glad you came in. Sit down, Margaret."

"What is it?"

"Please sit down."

Margaret sat down. Thomas got down on one knee.

"What are you doing?"

Thomas reached in his pocket. He pulled out a box.

"Margaret, I've been waiting for the right moment to do this. I think this is the perfect moment. Beautiful,

I fell in love with you the first time I saw you. I don't want to be alone any more. Would you complete me by becoming my wife?"

Tears formed in Margaret's eyes.

Ann said, "Well answer him, baby."

Margaret looked at her mother and then at Thomas.

Margaret said, "Yes, I'll marry you."

Thomas put the ring on her finger. He cupped her face with his hands and kissed her.

They stayed awhile longer with Ann. After they left the room, Margaret invited Thomas to her home. When they arrived, the babysitter was in the kitchen. Margaret introduced Thomas to her, and Thomas noticed the surprised expression on her face. After the babysitter left, Margaret went up to check on Ana. She was in bed but still awake.

"Hi, baby."

"Hi, Mommy."

"Come here, baby. There's someone I want you to meet."

"Who, Mommy?"

"Just come on."

Ana jumped into Margaret's arms. They went downstairs, and when Thomas saw them, he stood up.

"Ana, this is Mr. Gibson."

Ana shied away.

"Hi, Ana," Thomas said. "How are you?"

Ana smiled but continued to clutch Margaret.

"Okay," Margaret said. "Let's go to bed. Thomas, I'll be back."

Thomas said, "Nice to meet you, Ana. Bye."

Ana waived and said, "Good-bye."

Margaret came back downstairs a half hour later.

"So how do you think that went?" Thomas asked.

"She was okay. She'll be fine. Thomas, when did you want to get married?"

"Whatever date you choose. I just want to be with you."

"Okay. I would like my mother to be at our wedding. You know what that means, right?"

"I'm fine. Let's do this."

"Are you sure?"

"Yes. I am."

"How about next week? We'll have it in the hospital."

"What day?"

"Wednesday."

"Sounds good."

"Are you sure you're okay with this?"

Thomas pulled her to him and kissed her. He stayed until midnight going over the wedding plans.

The next day, Margaret got Ana up, and they dressed and had breakfast. During breakfast, Ana said, "You move fast, Mommy."

"Yes, baby. Mommy has a lot to do today. You know that nice man last night?"

"Yes, Mommy."

"Well Mommy's going to marry him."

"He's going to live here?"

This was the first time that she thought about living arrangements. She decided she would talk to Thomas about it later. "I don't know where we're going to live, baby."

After breakfast, Margaret took Ana with her to the florist. Then they went shopping for dresses for the wedding for the two of them and Ann. Margaret then took Ana to the church to see if her minister was available. He was. She met with Thomas for the three of them to have lunch together so Ana could get use to having Thomas around. Ana seemed to warm up to him. During the rest of the weekend, they called a few close friends to invite them. On Monday, Margaret and Thomas took the rest of the week off.

By Wednesday, everything had been arranged. Margaret and Ana went to the hospital to get dressed. At eleven, the flowers arrived. The minister showed up at 12:30, along with Thomas and his best man. The chapel had been decorated. They transported Ann to the chapel. Ana, who was the flower girl, entered the chapel, and then Dr. Stevens walked Margaret to the front of the chapel.

The minister began, "We are gathered here today to witness two souls coming together to make a vow of devotion to one another. It is rare to find two people as giving as these. As you know, today is not only special because two people have made the decision to become one, but this couple loves this woman," he motioned to Ann, "so much that they needed her to be a part of this momentous ceremony. Thomas Kincaid Gibson, do you take Margaret Ann Daniels to be your lawfully wedded wife, to honor, to cherish, to forsake all others till death do you part?"

"I do."

"Margaret Ann Daniels, do you take Thomas Kincaid Gibson to be your husband, to cling to him, honor, cherish, and forsake all others until death do you part?"

"I do."

"Who gives this woman?"

Ann said, "I do."

"Is there any reason that this man and woman should not get married? Speak now or forever hold your peace."

The minister paused.

"Thomas and Margaret, I now pronounce you man and wife. You may kiss your bride."

Thomas took Margaret into his arms and kissed her. Everyone clapped and then walked up to the couple and congratulated them. Thomas and Margaret went and hugged Ann.

As the group left the chapel, Ann was taken back to her room. A few people from the group went to Ann's room where refreshments were served. Everyone left after an hour. Margaret had the housekeeper take her car and Ana home. She and Thomas changed clothes at the hospital and then kissed Ann good-bye.

Thomas and Margaret went to stay at the Tropicana Casino and Hotel in Atlantic City. They had reserved the New Yorker Suite until Sunday. They walked on the boardwalk, shopped in the stores, got massages, went swimming in the hotel pool, and went to various shows. At night, they dined and savored each other's company. Each day, they called to check on both Ann and Ana.

On the last day, they discussed their living arrangements. They decided that for the time being, they would keep both homes. Thomas would move into Margaret's home; Margaret didn't want to do too much too fast. She wanted Ana to be able to adjust emotionally.

They checked out Sunday morning. Margaret wanted to stop by the hospital to see Ann before returning home. Ann was overjoyed to see them. After a little while, Thomas left to go to his home to gather up some clothes and personal items to take to Margaret's house.

While Thomas was gone, Ann said, "How was your honeymoon?"

"It was beautiful. It was so romantic."

"How is Ana taking it?"

"I think she's going to be okay. He made her laugh a few times, and she talks to him."

"That's good. Have you decided where you're going to live?"

"For now, we're going to stay in my house."

"How's his home? Is it big enough for a growing family?"

"He has three bedrooms, but it's not very large."

"Margaret, I was going to wait until I was gone and have them notify you, but I would like to give this to you and Thomas as a wedding gift. Hand me the manila envelope from that box."

Margaret handed Ann the envelope. Ann looked through the envelope and pulled out some papers. "I want you to have this as a wedding gift. When Thomas comes back, give it to him and he can add his name to it."

Margaret said, "Thank you." She looked at the paper Ann had given her. It was the deed to Ann's home. To Margaret's amazement, it had her name on it. She looked at Ann, wondering when Ann had done this. Margaret hugged her mother. Just then, Thomas walked into the room. He walked over to Margaret, noticing her watery eyes, and put his arm around her shoulders.

He said, "Are you all right?"

Margaret handed him the deed. He looked at it and then at Ann.

"I couldn't wait. I wanted you to have this as your wedding gift. Thomas, take care of it. I want you to put your name on it."

"Ann, are you sure?"

"Yes, you're starting a new life. Margaret was telling me about both of your homes. They don't seem large enough for a growing family. Also, I want it to be in both of your names. I want my home to become your home."

Thomas said, "Thank you."

"Thomas, I want you to jump right on this. I want to see the name change."

"I'll take care of it this week."

* * *

After he had gotten the name on the deed changed, Thomas brought it to Ann. The couple decided to rent their homes, rather than sell them. Once the deed had been changed over, Thomas and Margaret visited their new home. They surveyed the house and decided to change some of the rooms and remodel the kitchen. Although it was a beautiful kitchen, they wanted to make some personal changes. The basement was finished, but the couple decided to change a few things down there as well. The front yard was so beautifully manicured they couldn't imagine changing anything. Margaret actually felt Ann's presence there.

A month before they were to move in, all the changes had been made. That was when Ann died.

Margaret had gone to work. As usual, she checked in on Ann. Her vitals were weak. Margaret checked the chart and saw that her condition had been that way all night. She lingered in the room and then pressed the button for the nurse's station. The nurse, Betty, came in and asked if everything was all right. Margaret told her that everything was fine but asked Betty if she would take her shift. Betty agreed to make Margaret's rounds.

After Betty left, Margaret called Thomas and asked him to come to the hospital. He agreed to leave work. He didn't ask why; he dropped what he was doing and headed to the hospital. When he walked into the room, Margaret's head was on the bed next to Ann. He looked at the monitors and saw that Ann was still alive. He walked behind Margaret, bent down, and kissed her on the back of her head. He shifted her body in the chair, sat behind her, and put his arms around her. Within an hour, the machines quieted.

Margaret looked up at Ann. She watched to see if her chest was moving. She took her mother into her arms and cried. Thomas put his arms around her. Tears formed in his eyes. The doctor and nurses on duty quickly came into the room, including the crash team. Margaret looked up.

Holding Ann, she said, "No, let her go."

The team stood frozen. After a few minutes, they left the room. Margaret and Thomas were left alone with Ann. Margaret looked at Thomas and said, "She's gone. My mother's gone."

Thomas said, "She's not in any more pain. You know she would have loved to stay, but she couldn't any longer. She's with Mark now."

Margaret gently laid Ann down. She put her arms around Thomas, and he held her while she cried. Margaret sat and watched Ann as if somehow Ann might awaken. After an hour, Thomas said, "Beautiful, let me take you home. You need to get some rest."

Numb, Margaret allowed Thomas to lead her to the car. He fastened her seatbelt and then drove off. When they arrived at Margaret's house, Thomas picked her up and carried her up to bed. He undressed her, and she laid back. Thomas explained what had happened to the housekeeper, said goodnight to her, and then went to check on Ana. He then returned to their bedroom and got in bed. He pulled Margaret to him and held her. She finally fell asleep, her face wet with tears.

During the next two days, arrangements were made according to Ann's orders. The morning of the funeral, Margaret got out of bed, showered, dressed, and then went into Ana's room and washed her up and dressed her. When they went downstairs, they saw that Thomas had cooked breakfast. Margaret gave him a strained smile, and he walked over to her and kissed her. He playfully pinched Ana's check.

"Good morning," Ana said.

Thomas responded, "Good morning, sunshine."

After they finished breakfast, the limo arrived and they left for the church. To Margaret's surprise, as they entered the church, she saw the side for non-family members almost filled. Nearly a quarter of the people were the hospital staff. An hour had been set aside for the viewing, and when the viewing was over, the funeral service began. The minister stood up and read the Old Testament. The assistant minister read the New

Testament, and the organist played a melody while the soloist sang "Eyes on the Sparrow."

When they asked if there was anyone who would like to speak, an attractive woman with a slim figure went up to speak. Although she looked a little aged, Margaret didn't think that she was older than fifty. The woman identified herself as Candice, and Margaret caught her breath, feeling like she could have fallen out of her seat.

Candice said, "I was good friends with Ann many years ago. Many times when I was in a bind, she helped me. We lost contact a few years ago after her husband died. Probably because I didn't know what to say to her anymore. She had lost the love of her life. She was very sad. I know I should have kept in touch, but I was going through some things myself. If there was ever a beautiful person, Ann was it. She achieved so much." Candice looked at Margaret and continued, "Your mother loved you so much. I was thrilled when I read the obituary in the paper and saw that she had found you. I'm happy that her final days were with the most important person in her life. God bless you and your family."

As Candice headed to her seat, she stopped and hugged Margaret.

* * *

A month after the funeral, the Gibson finally moved into Ann's house. They had left all of the pictures that had been up with the original decorations. As Margaret went through the house, she entered the formal dining room and saw a picture of Mark and Ann. She did not remember seeing it before. They were a young couple who looked like they had a promising future. Margaret stared at her mother smiling. It was not a strained, sick, or aged smile, it was one of true happiness. She looked closely at Mark. He was more handsome than her mother had described. All of the coworkers and acquaintances of Mark's she had met at her mother's funeral has spoken so kindly of him. Margaret could see why her mother loved him so much. This was already her favorite room in the house.

Ana ran into the room, breaking Margaret's concentration. "There you are, Mommy. I was looking for you. Daddy showed me my room. I love it."

Margaret looked at Ana in amazement. She said, "Daddy? Is your father here?"

Ana responded, "Not that daddy, my other daddy."

Margaret had never heard Ana call Thomas "Daddy"; as a matter of fact, she realized, Ana had not called him anything.

When Thomas walked into the room, Ana ran up to Thomas and said, "I found her, Daddy."

Thomas picked Ana up and looked at Margaret. Margaret saw in his expression that this must have been the first time that he had heard it as well. Margaret smiled.

Thomas said to Ana, "I see." Turning to Margaret, he said, "Did Ana tell you she loves her room?"

"Yes, she did." Margaret said to Ana, "Your grand-mom helped decorate your room."

"She did? I miss Grand-mom."

Margaret said, "Me too, baby." She looked at Thomas. "Have you ever noticed this picture?"

"It used to be in the bedroom. After Mark died, it made Ann so sad that she took it down and put it in the basement. I guess the people who fixed the basement brought it up, cleaned it, and put it in here. It does go well in here."

* * *

Two years passed. Ana's father married Shirley, and they had a girl. Steve continued paying child support but stopped having visits with Ana. Ana and Thomas had become very close.

He would sit with Margaret while she read to Ana, and sometimes he would read stories to Ana at bedtime.

One day, Margaret got up for work and thought of calling in sick because she was very tired. She took a shower, and while she was getting dressed, Thomas woke up. He got out of bed, walked over to her, and put his arms around her.

"Good morning, beautiful," he said. "Are you feeling all right?"

"Yes. I'm just a little tired these days. I think I might be coming down with something."

"You should get yourself checked out. I don't want you getting sick."

"I'll make an appointment when I'm off again."

"I think you should do it sooner because you're not off for another week."

"Baby, let's talk about it later," she said. "I have to get to work."

"Okay. We're going to talk later." He kissed her and then released her.

Margaret grabbed a cereal bar and left. She ate it on the way to work. When she arrived at work, she parked the car and got out. She felt a little light headed. She shrugged it off because she figured that either she got up too quickly or she didn't have enough to eat. She figured she'd get something with a little more substance on her first break.

After making two of her rounds, she walked to the nurse's station to pick up a file. Just as she and Dr. Lee were passing each other, Margaret fainted. Dr. Lee broke her fall and called for help. Margaret was taken to one of the empty rooms. When she came to, Dr. Lee was standing over her.

Margaret said, "What happened?"

Dr. Lee said, "You fainted. Are you all right?"

"I can't believe I fainted."

"Let me check your vitals."

"I'm all right. I probably just need to eat."

"Even so, I want to check you out."

Dr. Lee checked Margaret's blood pressure, throat, ears, and chest. She took blood and asked for urine.

When the test results got back, Dr. Lee returned to where she had left Margaret resting.

"Mrs. Gibson, shame on you."

Margaret looked concerned. "What is it, Dr. Lee?"

"Everything looks good, but you need to take it easy. I want you to take the rest of the week off."

"What's wrong with me?"

"Nothing is wrong. You're going to have a baby."

Margaret looked at her in disbelief.

Dr. Lee continued, "I want you to go home. I've written you a prescription for prenatal vitamins."

"Dr. Lee, would you take me as a patient?"

"I would be honored. And since you're my patient now, I want you back to see me in a month."

Before Dr. Lee let Margaret leave, she took all the pertinent information concerning Margaret's medical history. After Margaret told Dr. Lee when her last period was, the doctor let Margaret hear the baby's heartbeat and pulled a picture of the baby up on the monitor, even though it was very tiny.

As Margaret drove home, she became excited. She talked to her mother as if she could hear her. When she arrived home, no one was there. Ana was still in school, and Thomas was at work. Margaret immediately went into the kitchen and fixed herself a big salad and an orange juice. She called Red Lobster and placed an order for pick up. Fifteen minutes later, she drove to pick it up. When she returned home, she fixed the dining room table. After checking everything over, Margaret went up to her bedroom and lay down.

Thomas came home after picking Ana up. He saw that Margaret's car was in the driveway, so he instructed Ana to go up to her room quietly. Thomas went into their room and saw Margaret asleep. He went over to her and put his wrist to her forehead. She awakened.

He said, "Sorry. I didn't mean to wake you."

"It's okay. What time is it?"

"Six o'clock."

"I meant to be up before now. I didn't realize I needed this much rest."

"How are you feeling?"

"Just tired."

"Did you call your doctor?"

"No."

"Margaret."

"Baby, it's okay. Are you hungry?"

"A little. Don't change the subject though."

"Baby, I'm fine." Margaret got out of bed. "I ordered some food. Get changed and come down for dinner." Margaret kissed him, smiled assuredly, and then left and went into Ana's room.

"Hi, baby."

"Hi, Mommy. Are you all right? Daddy said that you need your rest."

"Mommy's fine. You want to help me fix the dinner table?"

Ana jumped up. "Sure."

"Let's go."

The two went downstairs into the kitchen, and when Ana saw all the food Margaret had picked up, she said, "Wow."

"Let's take the food in the dinning room."

"Really?" said Ana.

They prepared the table. When Thomas came downstairs, he didn't see them in the kitchen, so he went into the dining room. "Wow!" he said. "What's the special occasion?"

"I wanted us to have a nice dinner," Margaret said.

They sat down, and after saying grace, they began to eat. Thomas kept glancing suspiciously at Margaret.

After they ate the main course, Margaret excused herself from the table. She returned with cheesecake, fresh fruit, and cool whip. Thomas looked at her, as her slice was larger than what she would normally eat. He watched as she ate it.

When they were finished eating, Margaret moved away from the table. She looked at Thomas and began, "I went to work today, but I was sent home." A worried look came over Thomas's face. "I fainted."

Thomas said, "What?"

Ana said, "Are you all right, Mommy?"

"I'm fine." Margaret smiled. "They ran tests. They said everything is good. I'm actually pretty healthy. They want me to stay home the rest of the week though."

"Are you sure everything's okay?" Thomas said. "Why do they want you to stay home?"

"I was told that I need to rest. I'm pregnant."

Thomas got up and briskly went to Margaret. He picked her up and swung her around. Then he stopped. "I'm sorry. Are you all right?"

"Baby, I'm fine."

"Are you sure? How many months?"

Simultaneously, Thomas and Margaret looked at Ana. She looked sad.

Margaret asked, "Are you okay, baby?"

"Mommy, are you and Daddy going to still love me?"

"Of course, baby. We could never stop loving you."

"Daddy did."

They knew what she meant.

Margaret went over to Ana and said, "Baby, your daddy didn't stop loving you. I can't explain why he stopped spending time with you. I guess he just got busy with his new family."

Thomas said, "Sunshine, I love you, and I would never stop loving you. You have a new family. I could be your one and only dad. Would you like that?" Thomas looked at Margaret. She understood what he was referring to and nodded her head.

Ana said, "How?"

"I can adopt you. That means you will be my daughter, like me and your mommy had you together. Your other daddy will no longer be your daddy."

Ana thought about it for a little while. Then she put her arms around Thomas's neck and said, "Yes."

The next day, Thomas put things in motion. Margaret reached out to Steve, Ana's biological father. It was two weeks later when Steve responded. He was hesitant at first, but a week later, he called Margaret and agreed to let Thomas adopt Ana.

* * *

Two months later, Ana was adopted by Thomas. Margaret cut her work hours, and they remodeled one of the rooms for the baby, including Ana in the whole process.

Margaret went on maternity leave two months before her due date. She got everything ready for the baby, and she made sure she spent time with Ana, discussing her feelings about her new family.

Two weeks before Margaret was due, Thomas cut his days down to half. They went on outings when Ana got out of school. On the day Margaret went into labor, the couple set it up for Ana to be at the hospital. After five hours of labor, Margaret delivered a six-pound, nine-ounce baby boy. Ana was escorted into Margaret's room before they brought the baby in. Ana smiled. She looked into the basinet and smoothed her hand over her baby brother's face. The baby smiled.

Ana said, "He likes me."

Margaret said, "Of course he likes you. You're his big sister."

"I'm a big sister." She bent down and kissed her baby brother.

Manufactured By: RR Donnelley
Momence, IL USA
September, 2010